CONTESTING

The People v. Wade and Wade

Andrew Kooman

Fair Winds Creative Co.

CONTENTS

AN EMPTY ROOM

Lights up on a WOMAN sitting on the floor in a stark room. Her knees are pulled into her body and she looks not at, but beyond, a MAN who lies near to her, motionless on the floor with his back to her.

They are both in boxer-like shorts and white T-shirts. Except for the light of two dull spots, they are otherwise surrounded by shadows.

The MAN wakes with a start, physically overwhelmed. He doesn't see the woman at first. He takes in his surroundings. When he gains what bearings he has, he turns and sees the WOMAN. He is frightened.

MAN Who are you?

WOMAN Take it easy.

MAN Where am I?

He stands up quickly and blacks out.

WOMAN Quiet. Don't move so fast.

She stands to stop him from falling.

MAN Where am I?

WOMAN Easy. You'll fall over. Just sit down and get it together. It's the effects of the drugs.

She helps him back to the ground.

MAN Drugs?

WOMAN That's what I figure.

He grabs his crotch and looks around, assessing things.

MAN We were drugged?

WOMAN I can't be certain.

MAN Do I know you?

WOMAN I don't know. Do you know me?

MAN I can't say.

WOMAN We must.

MAN Where the heck are we?

WOMAN Easy.

His sudden movement has made him nauseas.

How does it feel?

MAN Like a marching band is walking through my chest. And like an... an elephant shat in my mouth. Like a... cottony, dry, gritty taste and pain all over my body.

2

She laughs at this.

What?

WOMAN That's one way to say it.

MAN How long does it last?

WOMAN Not too long. But I wasn't jumping up and moving around like you. I just sat here.

MAN Doing what?

WOMAN Thinking.

MAN About what?

WOMAN Asking the same stupid questions as you.

MAN Stupid?

WOMAN And I waited for you to wake up.

MAN I'm in a fog.

WOMAN Yeah.

MAN Where are my pants?

WOMAN I don't know.

MAN Where are yours?

WOMAN I don't know that either.

MAN How long have you been sitting here?

WOMAN I'm not sure.

MAN Do you know anything?

WOMAN Better part of an hour?

MAN Just like that. Sitting there. Watching me and thinking.

WOMAN Pretty much, that's right.

MAN Did you try to find a way out of here?

WOMAN No.

MAN You didn't move?

WOMAN Something told me not to.

MAN Something?

WOMAN Ya.

MAN Like what?

WOMAN Something... I don't know, a knowing.

MAN Oh boy.

WOMAN Ya.

MAN Well what are you waiting for, let's try to get out of here!

> *He stands, staggers, moves toward the shadows.*

WOMAN I don't think you should be moving so quickly.

MAN Thanks for the concern but -

He is stopped by an invisible barrier at the edge of the shadow.

What the...

WOMAN What is it?

MAN That's strange.

He tries again.

I can't move.

WOMAN Paralysis?

MAN No

WOMAN I told you not to move so fast.

MAN No no no no no. Not paralysis. I can move. See?

He shows her he can move.

I can't move.

WOMAN It must be some type of sedative.

MAN I can't move beyond this point. Come here. There's a barrier or something.

He walks in the opposite direction toward the opposing shadows and is stopped at the fringe of light. She walks slowly toward him, puts out her hand and feels the invisible force.

WOMAN What's going on?

MAN I don't know. Where are we?

WOMAN I told you already I don't know! Stop asking me that!

MAN Ok ok ok. Just let me think.

WOMAN Yes. Think.

MAN Well...

WOMAN Well?

MAN Well, what do you remember?

WOMAN About what?

MAN About anything? I don't know. How we got here? Where this is? [To self] I... I don't remember anything.

WOMAN Me either. But -

MAN But what?

WOMAN I know you.

MAN You do?

WOMAN Yes. I do. Somehow I know that I know you because when I woke up, just like you, startled and afraid and my whole body was racked with pain like yours was. Your arm was around me, and I felt...

MAN What? Come on - what did you feel?

WOMAN Comforted.

MAN You did?

WOMAN Yes. I wouldn't feel like that if I didn't know who you are.

This comforts him.

He reaches out his hand, an impulse to touch her. She evades it, stepping away from him.

We were lovers.

MAN Lovers?

WOMAN Yes. We were lovers.

MAN Were?

WOMAN Yeah.

MAN Here?

WOMAN No. Before.

At her assurance, the THUD of a sound is heard and the circle of light they find themselves in expands. A FIRST OBJECT is revealed.

What was that?

MAN I'm not sure. Hello?

They wait for a response. The MAN reaches out his hand tentatively to where he had been blocked from moving further and his hand surpasses the invisible boundary line.

Did you see that?

WOMAN See what?

MAN I can move past it. Look.

> *He walks forward and isn't stopped.*

See?

> *He keeps walking but is stopped again at the edge of the shadow. He looks at the WOMAN and marches to the opposite fringe. He is stopped at the new shadow line.*

You?

> *She tries, going to first one, then another point along the circumference of the shadow. She is stopped but it is then she notices the object on the floor.*

WOMAN What's this?

MAN We're trapped, that's what this is.

WOMAN No, look. There's something here, in a cloth bag.

> *She walks over, picks it up.*

MAN What are you doing?

WOMAN Seeing what it is.

MAN You don't know where it came from.

WOMAN So?

MAN Doesn't it concern you that it just appeared?

Not here one moment, then...here?

WOMAN Seems to be a trend in this place. Well?

A GAS MASK

She hands the bag to him. After some thought he takes it. He puts the bag onto the floor, opens the draw strings and pulls out a gas mask.

I hate the sight of those things.

MAN They always remind me of -

WOMAN Paris?

MAN Yes.

WOMAN The whole city.

MAN One moment it was here.

WOMAN And then it was just...

MAN Gone.

WOMAN Think we're in a bunker?

MAN Could be.

WOMAN Another nuke?

MAN If we are, we're far enough away. We obviously had enough time to get here.

WOMAN But then where is everyone else? Our clothes?

MAN Food, water -

WOMAN No, this isn't a bunker. It's more like a prison

MAN A jail cell.

WOMAN But why? And for what?

MAN [Moving to the outskirt of shadows, yelling] Hey. Can anybody hear us? We demand to speak to our lawyers!

Silence.

WOMAN We have lawyers?

MAN Well if we don't, we should.

The WOMAN puts on the mask and presses it against the contours of her face, adjusts the straps.

What are you doing?

WOMAN Trying it on.

MAN Take it off!

WOMAN Why?

MAN What are you doing?

WOMAN I'm trying the mask on. What if they gas us?

MAN What if who gases us?

WOMAN Well there's a reason this mask was left on the floor.

MAN Then take it off!

WOMAN No.

MAN So you live and I die?

He moves to take the mask off. She straight-arms him. He stops.

WOMAN Settle down! I just want to see if it works.

She rips it off her head, astonished.

Can't I do that?

MAN There's only one mask.

WOMAN I see that. That's why we need to know if the seal works.

MAN So it works, and you get to use it?

WOMAN How chivalrous of you to offer. I use it. You use it. We can pass it between us on full lungs of good air, if each of us takes a turn with it, if the gas in the room isn't harmful and can't be absorbed through our skin. Didn't you attend any of the free disaster workshops offered on every street corner after the first bomb went off?

MAN Sorry. It was just...

WOMAN Can I?

MAN Please.

She slips on the mask and adjusts the straps. She squeezes the nozzle and blows air out in two quick exhalations. She puts her hand on the filter and sucks air in.

WOMAN It's good. A good vacuum. It'll work.

MAN You sure?

She pulls the mask off.

WOMAN Geez, you didn't learn anything from Paris, did you?

MAN Just to stop trusting people, and fend for myself. Pas de tout.

WOMAN I had a husband like you once.

MAN Really?

WOMAN I don't know. I mean, I could have. Those words just sorta popped out of my mouth.

MAN But look, we're remembering things, without trying.

WOMAN Like what?

MAN Like your husband. What was his name?

WOMAN I don't know if there was a husband. It was just something to say.

He grabs her hand.

Hey -

MAN Easy -

WOMAN Don't touch me.

MAN Look. You can tell, you wore a ring. You were married.

WOMAN Or I just wore a ring.

MAN Good point.

WOMAN I mean, where are my clothes? My things? We don't know anything about anything? This is a bad dream I can't wake up from.

MAN Paris. We remember Paris! We both did, when we saw the mask.

WOMAN That's true.

MAN Ok. Let's just focus on that. What do you remember about it?

WOMAN I don't know... that it was bad.

MAN Yeah.

WOMAN It was... all over the news.

MAN Every day

WOMAN On every feed. It was every headline on every paper. You couldn't escape the horror of it. The images they kept playing over and over. I couldn't stand it, but I couldn't turn away from it.

MAN Me too.

WOMAN The complete absence of blood.

MAN What did you say?

WOMAN There was no blood! No trace of the carnage. No bodies. At ground zero everything was just - gone. Like every one and everything had been blown through the earth.

MAN Blown or incinerated.

WOMAN And for awhile, no one could say exactly how it happened or why or even what it was, but we all knew.

MAN A suitcase nuke.

WOMAN We just didn't know where the first one would go off.

MAN I remember thanking God.

WOMAN Thanking?

MAN Yes. That it wasn't us. It was a terrible, selfish prayer, but I meant it. I thought we would be hit first - I was sure of it. No one really hates the French. We all pretend we do but we know they - the terrorists - all hate us.

Those first few days, after the bomb. Do you remember that?

WOMAN Sort of.

MAN I mean real terror. A line of fear, like - what - like a line of rebar forced through the skull, through my brain and into my heart...

out the abdomen, just impaling - I don't know, disemboweling - and sticking me to the ground.

WOMAN I don't want to remember this! Of all things this.

MAN I was frozen in fear. Couldn't go to work for more than a month - didn't even call the boss - because every briefcase had a bomb. Everyone around me could be a terrorist.

And if it went off on the subway or in the street or a block away in some high rise you couldn't duck for cover or be shielded from the blow, you'd just [beat] incinerate.

I don't want to incinerate.

WOMAN I was pregnant. When the bomb went off, I was pregnant and I thought -

MAN How can we bring a child into this world?

WOMAN Yes

There is a THUD of a sound and the circle of light they find themselves expands again. A SECOND OBJECT can be seen in the new circumference of light, but neither of them see it yet.

They stare at each other, long. He breaks from her gaze first.

MAN The lights again. Did you notice that?

He walks around the space.

There's more room. See? The space we're in... it's...

expanding somehow. Systematically?

WOMAN What did you say?

MAN The room, it's getting bigger.

WOMAN I know that. I mean - what did you say just then?

MAN Feel around. Maybe there's a way outa here.

They circle the space. He more intently than her. Her mind is pushing against a door of significant memory that she can't quite open. He kicks a SMALL OBJECT on the floor accidentally. It rolls across the room. He watches it. She doesn't notice.

Anything?

WOMAN No, but...

MAN What?

WOMAN It's like I'm starting to see.

MAN See what?

He walks to the object while she thinks. She suddenly grabs her temples in pain.

WOMAN Through the fog... through my - in my memory. In my mind.

MAN You are? That's good.

He picks the OBJECT up. She turns and looks at him, pointing. He hides the OBJECT behind his back instinctively.

WOMAN Like when you were speaking just then.

MAN Then?

WOMAN Yes, about Paris.

MAN Oh that. I didn't mean it.

WOMAN Really?

MAN No. I didn't want any of those people to die. I wasn't happy about it.

WOMAN No. Not that. What you said about the baby.

MAN What baby?

WOMAN Mine. When I told you I was pregnant.

MAN What are you talking about?

WOMAN When I said - when... when I remembered that I was pregnant when the bomb, when it went off in Paris, you said -

MAN I don't even know what I said.

WOMAN Just then, before the lights got brighter! You said, "How can we bring a child into this world?"

MAN So.

WOMAN So?

MAN What does it matter? I just said it. Like you or anyone says anything.

WOMAN But I've heard those words before. I know I have.

MAN Everyone has. It's a shit world. Anyone whose ever brought a baby into it has probably said those exact same words.

WOMAN But I've heard you say those words before.

MAN Me?

WOMAN Yes

MAN No that's... that's impossible. You're memory's all wonky.

> *She touches her hand to her head.*

WOMAN Well, I can't disagree with that. I don't like it, though.

MAN Me either.

WOMAN I don't like it!

MAN Look.

> *He holds out the object in his hand.*

WOMAN What is it?

MAN I don't know. I found it, just now, with the lights. Kicked it across the floor.

> *She reaches to hold it, but he steps out of the way so she can't.*

In your haze you've been confusing me for someone else, you know.

WOMAN You should see what's there.

MAN I will.

WOMAN Well, what are you waiting for?

MAN I'm just thinking things through.

WOMAN What's there to think about? How it got here?

MAN Not how. When. The mask came with the lights.

WOMAN And that loud sound. It frightened me, both times.

MAN Do you think they fell?

WOMAN From where?

MAN I don't know, the sky?

WOMAN We're in a room.

MAN Are we for sure?

> *They both look up, wince at the lights.*

WOMAN That's too small - too light to make that kind of sound from falling.

MAN True. But you're right. This came with the sound. And with the lights. So did the mask.

WOMAN So what does that mean?

MAN I don't know. But at least we're starting to know something. We're collecting things.

WOMAN A gas mask and -

MAN and facts. To explain these phenomena.

WOMAN Phenomena?

MAN This... space.

WOMAN You think we're out in space?

MAN Outer space? No! We're just here.

WOMAN You're sounding all funny about it.

MAN Well this is a funny business we're caught up in.

WOMAN I'll say. You know what's really funny?

MAN No.

WOMAN You not opening that. What are you waiting for?

MAN Alright!

He slowly opens the box.

WOMAN Well?

MAN It's a necklace.

WOMAN Let's see.

He pulls out a silver chain and holds it up.

A LOCKET

MAN Wait, it's a locket. A heart-shaped locket.

At seeing it she instinctively clutches her neck. She steps away, turning her back to him to think.

WOMAN Don't open it yet.

MAN Why?

WOMAN Just don't. Just wait. I gotta think. It's familiar.

He examines it closely.

MAN Hmm. This is strange. It looks like the clamp on the back is missing. Yeah. Look here. There's a link of chain on each side that's broken. There's no clasp. You couldn't wear it if you wanted to.

WOMAN I think I know what's inside.

MAN You do? How?

WOMAN A photograph.

MAN Well, that's a given.

WOMAN What I mean is, that I think I know what's in there, so I should tell you before you open it, because if I'm right, then... well... that's significant, see? It means that my memory - our memories - are coming back.

MAN So, who is it then? Who's on the photo in here?

WOMAN I don't know his name. But it'll be a.. a brown-eyed boy. About six years old.

MAN That's it?

WOMAN I can almost see his face. If I - if I close my eyes.

MAN So, can I open it now?

WOMAN Yes.

He opens it.

Well?

MAN You're wrong.

WOMAN What?

MAN Sorry.

WOMAN Who is it then?

MAN No one. It's empty.

WOMAN Empty? But -

She takes it from his hand.

MAN Nothing's there. So, I guess you could've been

right. Maybe someone took out the boy's photo.

She offers it back to him.

No, you keep it.

She takes the box it came with and puts the locket back inside, snapping the lid shut. With the snap, she looks startled at the man, who has gone over to the gas mask and picked it up.

WOMAN David.

He looks at her and in the same moment there is more light and a loud THUD.

He is startled by the sound and light and her intense gaze and starts to look around the room at the space.

She walks over to him with purpose.

That's your name. David.

MAN No it's not.

WOMAN But it is! It just came to me, like a... like a lightening bolt. Striking me in the dark. Boom. Just like these lights. You're David.

MAN That's not my name.

WOMAN Then what is it?

MAN I don't know, but -

WOMAN If you don't know what your name is how can you be so sure what it isn't?

MAN I'd know if it was. When you said it, I'd know that.

WOMAN But the lights.

MAN What about the lights?

WOMAN The sound. Yes. Don't you see? With the sound. With the lights! There's more space, too.

He feels around the illuminated space.

MAN You're right. I mean... about the space. It's bigger. Ah!

He shakes his head, then grabs it in pain.

WOMAN What?

MAN My head! Ow!

WOMAN A fog?

MAN A bloody painful one. I can

WOMAN almost remember?

MAN It's like it's on the edge of my mind about to fall right into the place that makes things make sense. Feel that.

WOMAN What?

MAN Touch me. My forehead. My arm. It's like when I touch my body it feels bigger than it actually is. Can you feel that too?

WOMAN Not really

MAN And... and - close your eyes!

WOMAN David.

MAN When I close my eyes I can see myself and see this room as bigger than they are. What the heck is going on?

WOMAN David, calm down!

MAN My name is not David!

Lights and THUD. They both are completely still when they hear it.

From where they stand, they both survey the room. He stops when he sees her staring at something. He follows her gaze. There are TWO OBJECTS on the floor.

They both look back at each other. Slowly they walk to the centre of the space to the new objects. They each stand over one of them, pick them up. He holds an envelope. She holds a leather bound picture frame that opens like a book.

AN ENVELOPE AND
A PICTURE FRAME

MAN Ladies first.

*She slowly opens the book and when she sees the photo she
drops it immediately in shock.*

What?

Frantic, she takes a few steps back.

What's come over you?

He picks up the case.

WOMAN No!

*When she sees him reaching over to pick it up she quickly
grabs it and takes it to the edge of the light.*

MAN What's gotten over you?

WOMAN Leave me alone!

MAN Easy. What was in that?

WOMAN None of our business!

MAN Is it now.

WOMAN Leave me alone. Can't you see it's disturbed me? That it's pained me? Just leave it alone!

He steps to the other side of the space, away from her.

MAN I can't see what would disturb you so much. But I see that it's triggered you. Some sort of bad memory?

He steps toward her excitedly. She defensively clutches the object and hides it.

It's a good sign, though, isn't it? Even if it's painful. Yes, don't you see. Your memory is coming back. No pain, no gain...

He looks at the envelope in his hand. Opening it, he takes out a photograph, when he sees it he drops to his knees.

It's the boy.

Shift.

He has brown hair and brown eyes, just like you said.

He touches the photograph tenderly.

David?

Revelation.

My son.

He looks over to the woman and holds the photograph to her, a gesture that transforms her countenance. She is pulled to him and to the photograph as if by a tractor beam.

WOMAN Your son?

MAN Yes

WOMAN How do you know?

MAN I just do.

WOMAN Where is he?

MAN I don't know.

WOMAN What do you know?

MAN That I love him. Nothing more. What about you?

WOMAN I don't know anything either.

MAN This isn't the look of a woman who doesn't know anything. You know something!

WOMAN I don't.

MAN What is it?

WOMAN [Screaming] I want out of here! Let me out of here!

He walks over to her and hauls her by the arm.

MAN Do you know something about my David?

WOMAN [To the darkness] Why are you keeping us here?

MAN What do you know?

WOMAN Let us out!

She shields herself from him, afraid. He lets her go.

MAN [Shouting beyond the room] I need to see my son! I need to know he's alright!

He clutches his head in pain.

Something terrible has happened. [To her] Hasn't it?

WOMAN I think so.

MAN [Shouting to the darkness] What happened to David?

Only silence.

I have a son. And his name is David.

WOMAN Is?

MAN Yes. Is. Why would you ask such a thing?

WOMAN Think about where we are. If a bomb went off out there -

MAN Shut up!

WOMAN If a bomb went off out there and we're in here, alone -

MAN No, shut up! We don't know what happened.

She shrugs her shoulders.

I sure don't. What are you hiding from me - there - what are you hiding there that makes you so sure?

WOMAN A bitter memory. That's all. Trust me, okay?

MAN How do I know if I can? If I should?

WOMAN Trust me.

Silence.

Listen. We need to try to remember other things. You're right. We're starting to piece things together. But there's not really a pattern, is there, to our remembering?

MAN I don't know how we go about doing it.

WOMAN What did you do... for work... before you woke up here. Before the first nuke, the one we can remember, in Paris?

MAN I don't know.

WOMAN Come on. Think about it.

MAN I told you I can't remember anything.

WOMAN You already described some of it.

MAN I did? When?

WOMAN Before - you said you rode the subway or something.

MAN What does that matter?

WOMAN It matters a lot. I want to know who I'm in this God-forsaken cell with. Remembering what we did can help us tell what kind of...

MAN What?

WOMAN What kind of person... what kind of people we are.

MAN How do I remember?

WOMAN Think about your routine. About what you did every day, on the way to work. Think about the subway.

He closes his eyes. He takes a deep breath. He opens his eyes again after awhile.

MAN This is stupid.

WOMAN Just try!

MAN I did

WOMAN And?

MAN And what? Now I'm supposed to know my job title and the name of my employer?

WOMAN I'm not expecting that. Didn't you see anything, in your memory?

MAN Just a number.

WOMAN What number?

MAN A red number... an alarm clock! 5-5-5. AM.... that's when I woke up. In the mornings.

WOMAN To go to work?

MAN To get ready for work. 5:55. I'd set the alarm for 6:00 a.m., actually, but I always woke up five minutes before. Because I hate the sound of my alarm clock. It's that Neeah neeeeah neeah neeah -

WOMAN Ok! I got it. Why wouldn't you just buy a new one... with a different sound?

MAN I don't know.

WOMAN So you had a pretty standard routine, it sounds like.

MAN I guess.

WOMAN Up early every morning.

MAN Sure

WOMAN So you woke up... then what'd you do?

MAN I ate breakfast.

WOMAN Okay, then...

MAN Then the three S's.

WOMAN The three S's?

MAN Shit, shower and shave.

WOMAN Oh.

MAN Then the subway.

WOMAN So 4 S's.

MAN I guess so

WOMAN Do you remember what station you got on, or off?

He closes his eyes again.

MAN No. I just see a few random pictures in my mind.

WOMAN What are they?

MAN Boy you're relentless!

WOMAN Well?

MAN The man with the newsstand who I bought a paper from in the mornings between trains. He wore a wool hat and was missing a molar that I could see when he smiled after I paid.

WOMAN That's good. What else?

MAN The glass sky rise where I think I worked. Yeah, it must be. Reflective blue glass. And... and the courtyard below with two large birch trees.

WOMAN What city?

MAN I don't know.

WOMAN Well, we're getting somewhere. Anything

else?

He closes his eyes again.

MAN   Huh.   A   beautiful   brown   alligator   skin briefcase. The softest leather. I loved the feel of that in my hands.

WOMAN You were a lawyer.

MAN Yes

WOMAN Corporate?

MAN Criminal law

WOMAN District attorney's office

MAN The briefcase was a gift from my mother when I passed the bar.

He opens his eyes, smiling delight.

How did you know I practiced law?

WOMAN The memory came to me too. I remember that briefcase.

MAN You do?

WOMAN There was a silk pocket, sewn into the inside of it, in one of the compartments, where you kept a white slip of paper

MAN That I pulled from a fortune cookie

WOMAN At one of your favourite Chinese places near Central Park. You're not superstitious

MAN I'm not?

WOMAN but you kept it.

MAN I did?

WOMAN Yes.

MAN How do you know?

WOMAN I just know.

MAN What did the fortune say?

WOMAN What does it matter what it said? I don't know. Maybe it should've said you'd find yourself with no memory, locked up in a strange cave at the end of the world with the woman you proposed to on the same night you cracked open that fortune cookie.

> *She's surprised at the revelation.*

MAN Proposed?

WOMAN Yes.

He tries to absorb this information. As they stand in silence a HISSING SOUND can be heard. A mist starts to appear from the darkness and fill the space.

MAN Gas!

WOMAN Get the mask!

They both run for it. He gets to it first, grabs it. She looks at him, afraid. He hands it to her.

MAN You use it first. If I don't make it -

She grabs it, fumbles with it to get it on quickly. He takes an enormous breath. She steps toward the shadows, away from him.

He walks to the photo of David, picks it up and hugs it to his chest. He moves through the space, waving the mist with one hand and feeling for her. When he finds her, she mimes moving the mask and giving it to him.

He refuses.

She signals again but he grabs her hands instead and pulls her arms around his body into an embrace.

WOMAN What are you doing?

At the end of his breath, unable to hold it any more, he inhales deeply.

MAN It's better you live!

He starts to cough. She moves to help him. He pushes her away and falls to the ground on his hands and knees. The smoke starts to dissipate. They both wait for him to die.

WOMAN Nothing's happening.

MAN Sorry to disappoint you.

WOMAN Are you alright? Do you feel anything?

MAN Like an idiot - a light-headed one - for holding my breath so long.

WOMAN Burning in the lungs?

MAN No.

WOMAN Pain... in your abdomen or chest?

MAN No.

WOMAN Open your mouth.

He does, obediently. She looks him over, in his mouth, eyes, ears. She pulls off the mask.

MAN What are you doing?

WOMAN Well, you're fine. Why shouldn't I be?

She grabs her throat and screams.

MAN What what what what?

She stops screaming. Starts laughing.

WOMAN Sorry.

MAN That's not funny.

WOMAN A little humour at the end of the world. You should've seen the look on your face.

MAN Ha ha.

WOMAN It's colder in here.

MAN What happened?

WOMAN I don't know, but the temperature sure dropped.

MAN I can see that.

He looks at her chest. She folds her arm over her breasts.

WOMAN I'm freezing.

MAN Come here.

He hugs her to himself and starts to rub her arms, her back.

How's that?

WOMAN Better.

MAN There you go Honey.

WOMAN Honey?

She steps out of his embrace.

MAN Isn't that what I call you?

WOMAN Not anymore.

MAN No? How do you know that?

WOMAN Because I don't like it.

MAN You're my wife.

WOMAN Are?

MAN Yes.

WOMAN Was.

There is a THUD and another OBJECT drops from the roof,
suspended on a wire.

Here we go. They're playing with us.

MAN Who is?

WOMAN If it wasn't gas, what was it?

MAN I don't know.

WOMAN It was a test. The people keeping us here are starting to play games with us now that we're starting to remember things. We're like mice in their trap.

MAN What is it this time?

A BODY BAG

WOMAN A body bag.

MAN It can't be.

She steps closer to it.

Wait, what are you doing?

WOMAN I want to see what's inside.

MAN But it might be a body.

WOMAN That's usually what they're for.

MAN Leave it alone. It's...

WOMAN Unsanitary?

MAN No, it's more than that.

She slowly unzips the bag, peeks inside. He braces himself.

WOMAN Well, what do you know. No body here. It's clothes.

MAN Maybe it's our clothes.

She brings it to the centre into the light.

Maybe they're gonna let us out of here.

She reaches in to pull out two sets of prison coveralls. One blue, one pink, fit to their respective sizes.

WOMAN I don't think so. You're the attorney. What do these look like to you?

He hands the pink one to her.

This seems like a sexist cliché.

MAN You gonna put yours on?

WOMAN I don't know.

MAN It'll keep you warm.

WOMAN I don't like the optics of it.

MAN What optics?

WOMAN Us putting them on.

MAN We don't even know who's watching us - that is if anyone is watching us. Plus, I'm cold. My balls have crawled up into my abdomen and are quickly making their way to my armpits to keep warm.

WOMAN If we put them on it's like we're admitting to something.

MAN We are. We're admitting we're cold.

He pulls on the suit.

[Yelling to whomever] Whoever's out there, I'll just have you know that by putting on this jumpsuit, I'm confessing to my coldness and nothing else, in hopes that my balls will once again return to their intended place.

He models it for her, strutting around. She reads the number on his chest (which also appears in lettering on the back of the jumpsuit).

WOMAN Number 00011. You look like a prisoner to me.

MAN And I look like I could use a partner in crime. They're warm. He grabs his crotch, feels around exaggeratedly, mimes relief.

Really warm. [To his balls] Welcome back, boys! [To her] Look, you're shivering. Stop being so darn stubborn.

She reluctantly puts the coveralls on. She starts to rub her arms and legs when outfitted. Finally she stands content.

MAN That's better, huh? Number 00013. Lucky number.

WOMAN I thought you weren't superstitious.

MAN You said that, not me.

WOMAN I did?

MAN Yeah. Before the smoke. You think we were really married?

She looks at her ring finger and rubs it.

WOMAN Yes, I do.

MAN But that we're not anymore?

WOMAN Question is... Why did I leave you? For unfaithfulness?

She looks around the room, expecting an increase in lights.

MAN Who's to say you're the one who filed for divorce?

WOMAN Let's be real here.

MAN Excuse me?

WOMAN [Toward the darkness] Irreconcilable differences?

MAN [Toward the darkness] She was unfaithful to me?

WOMAN Cruelty?

MAN Refusing conjugal rights? [Beat] I can't think of any other reasons. Why else do people divorce?

WOMAN You're the lawyer.

MAN And what about David? He's... he's yours.

WOMAN You don't know that.

MAN David, he's mine too. He's our son.

THUD and more lights. A display board with her number, unlit, appears.

WOMAN This is a bad dream. For all we know, we're making all of this up!

MAN You were pregnant, with David, when the nuke went off on the Champs-Élysées.

THUD and more light. A board with his number, unlit, appears.

WOMAN How can you know that? I don't know that.

MAN You're the mother of my child.

THUD with increased light. A strange pod appears. It looks like an incubator. The glass medical device could enclose an adult.

A POD

WOMAN What is that?

Silence.

WHAT IS THAT?

MAN We both know.

WOMAN How did it get here?

MAN I don't know.

WOMAN What's that doing here?

MAN It's for us!

WOMAN How do you know that?

MAN Look at the leather straps.

WOMAN What do you mean "us"?

MAN Look at our numbers on the wall.

WOMAN So?

MAN Look at the numbers on our backs.

WOMAN These aren't our clothes. We just put them
on.

MAN They're meant for us. This is an MAiD chamber.

WOMAN There's only one pod.

MAN God help us.

WOMAN [Toward the darkness] Let me out of here!

MAN God. Help us!

WOMAN [Toward the darkness] I said let me out!

MAN What have we done that we're here?

WOMAN [Toward the darkness] This is inhumane. This is unnatural. This is wrong of you! You won't get away with this!

MAN There's been some misunderstanding! Yes. Please, let us talk with someone to clear things up!

WOMAN Clear things up? You think we can reason with them - whoever is holding us here?

MAN [Toward the darkness] Tell us what we've done!

WOMAN [Toward the darkness] I've done nothing wrong!

MAN No?

WOMAN That's right. Nothing.

MAN And yet you're here.

WOMAN So are you. I have a clear conscience.

MAN That's no defence!

WOMAN My conscience tells me I've done nothing.

MAN Who do you think we're standing before, God?

He stops at his own words.

Wait a minute.

WOMAN What?

MAN That's it! We're ... standing before the throne of God!

WOMAN That doesn't look like what I'd imagine his throne to be.

MAN "He will... judge the living and the dead."

WOMAN In pink jumpsuits? Maybe you were gassed just then.

MAN Are we Presbyterians? Is this the judgement?

WOMAN Where are the angels, then, huh? The saints. Where's everybody else?

MAN Maybe they're in... in similar purgatories. Awaiting their own fates as well. We could be Catholics.

WOMAN So you're, what, number 11 of all of humankind?

MAN Maybe I am!

WOMAN You'd be nearer the back of the bus I think.

MAN You got a better explanation then, Ms. Pink Jumpsuit?

WOMAN I don't.

MAN You and your clear conscience.

WOMAN What's that supposed to mean?

MAN You don't look like someone with a clear conscience to me.

WOMAN Don't point your finger at me.

MAN The way you freaked out when you looked at whatever was in that portfolio.

She steps toward it. He steps in front of her.

See?

WOMAN Leave it.

MAN What's in it that's so disturbing?

WOMAN Nothing - it's just... it's personal.

MAN Personal?

She walks around him but he pivots and gets to it before she can. He picks it up. He opens it and upon seeing what's inside snaps it quickly shut. He looks at her, a mix of shock and horror.

WOMAN Listen... I don't know what you're thinking right now, but let me explain.

He storms over to the photo he's dropped on the floor and picks it up.

MAN Explain? Yeah, you've got some explaining to do.

He sets the portfolio down and pulls out an 8x10 photograph, the same size as the one from the envelope. He picks both up at the same time and holds them for her to see. They are the same photo of the same brown-eyed boy. She starts to cry.

Where is he?

WOMAN I don't know.

MAN What happened to David?

WOMAN Get away from me!

MAN Look at me. Something terrible has happened, hasn't it?

WOMAN Yes.

MAN Something horrific.

WOMAN Yes.

He retreats from her. He is stopped by the wall but would run far from her if he could. He mumbles what he can remember.

MAN [To self, but the WOMAN can hear] I woke up, and I was over there. She was here the whole time. My head, and the sound in my ears, that taste in my mouth.... Think think think think

think.

There was Paris, we both remember that. The bomb and the briefcase and my boy. No no no no no there's more there's gotta be more.

[To WOMAN] What aren't you telling me?

WOMAN I don't know.

MAN What do you mean you don't know?

WOMAN I don't know what I'm not telling you. I don't know if I'm hiding something! I don't know what to say! All I know is when I saw that photograph I was afraid. A terror came over me, something terrible.

And it's still here. Still in the room with me, that terror. Sinking on my heart like a ship at sea with a hole in it, taking everything with it down to the bottom.

MAN What do you know?

WOMAN What you know as well as I do. It's a deep, sinking feeling. I can't say it.

MAN David, he's -

WOMAN Don't. Don't say anything.

MAN Okay then

WOMAN Don't say it!

MAN I won't.

WOMAN Thank you.

He holds the picture. Looks at it long and mournfully.

MAN So this is where we are. Where you can't escape the grief and the hurt of a thing.

WOMAN It's cruelty to let us drown in it, with no understanding... with no other memory.

MAN Sure doesn't explain that mask...

WOMAN or the chair for that matter.

MAN I can see your trace in him.

WOMAN What?

She walks over to him. Looks at the photograph.

MAN Your shape in him.

WOMAN There must be a way out of here.

MAN You want to hatch an escape?

WOMAN If we put our minds together.

MAN I know the way out.

WOMAN Where?

MAN It's through that pod

WOMAN God didn't give us brains to sit here idle.

The statement makes them both pause.

MAN Your father used to say that.

WOMAN He did?

MAN Or -

WOMAN He did -

MAN you used to tell me that your father used to say that all the time

WOMAN when I was a child. You're right.

MAN He pushed you all your life because he wanted you

WOMAN to be a doctor just like he was.

MAN And he got his wish.

WOMAN He did.

This memory wearies her.

MAN We had different childhoods.

WOMAN Everyone does.

MAN We came from different worlds. It drove you crazy.

WOMAN What's that supposed to mean?

MAN In our life - between us. Raising a child. We were so different, you and I.

WOMAN Were?

MAN Yeah, we were opposites. Magnetic poles. And yet we -

WOMAN Attracted?

MAN I guess. And stuck.

Mimes two magnets coming together.

WOMAN Well that sounds lovely.

MAN It was.

WOMAN Really? Was it really lovely?

MAN Yes.

WOMAN Well look at you, just free-flowing right now.

MAN We met in a hotel.

WOMAN Oh, here we go.

MAN I was naked.

WOMAN Okay. Let's stop this.

MAN No, wait. I'm remembering this.

WOMAN I'm not.

MAN You should. Boy, it was so embarrassing at the time.

WOMAN Gee, I can't imagine why...

MAN We had never met, and there I was...

WOMAN naked?

MAN Locked out of my hotel room. I was standing

there, in my socks and running shoes -

WOMAN Naked in the hallway?

MAN As the moon. I was alone, sorta panicking

WOMAN Well, yeah

MAN pleading with the door to open, because there was no one else inside the room and

WOMAN In just your running shoes? How did that happen?

MAN I don't know. I think I was going out for a jog, or had just come back from one

WOMAN Without shorts on?

MAN No, there was a good reason for it.

WOMAN I'll bet

MAN That was the funniest part of it all, but I can't remember it. And then you appeared.

WOMAN There's no way this is a love at first sight story

MAN You were leaving your room to head to the lobby. And here I was, this naked, stranded fool, covering myself with my hands, locked out of my room in that lonely hall. You got me a robe, from your room so that I could visit the concierge with some dignity. And... later that night

WOMAN Oh no no no no

MAN Later that night you returned to your room

WOMAN Please don't say that you were still naked

MAN And there was a lovely bouquet of flowers waiting for you, with a basket of fruit and a note that said,

MAN and WOMAN TOGETHER "To my heroine in the hallway."

MAN That's how we first met.

WOMAN That sounds memorable.

MAN We had lots of memorable times. We were... well, we were -

WOMAN We're not "were" yet. We're still alive -

MAN Well, I just mean -

WOMAN You can be "were"... but I'm - I'm gonna be "am". I am getting out of here.

MAN Okay, genius. You just go and save the day and use all your smarts.

WOMAN Are you picking a bone with me?

MAN No.

WOMAN Is this some old, recycled lovers' argument that you're remembering that I have no recollection of too?

MAN What are you talking about?

WOMAN That tone - yes, tone. That reflex, muscle memory laundry list of gripes you were just about to pull out.

MAN Umm... I was just saying that the odds are sort of stacked against you and your "way out" of here.

WOMAN Let's just cut the nostalgia and think about the present, because whether what we're remembering is true or not, I'm more worried about how we're going to avoid that death chamber.

MAN Okay

She gets busy looking around the room.

But it's just like you, you know, to say that.

She stops cold in her tracks.

WOMAN Really lover boy? You're gonna keep walking that line while I try to get us out of here?

She gets back to exploring the room and he stops to watch her in wonder.

MAN You're amazing.

WOMAN You bet I am!

MAN So doggone sure of yourself. We're locked in a jail cell at the end of the world and you're still gonna find a way out. All on your own.

WOMAN And you can send me a bouquet of flowers to thank me for rescuing you again. But please, this time keep your clothes on.

He watches her until she becomes self conscious and

ultimately gives up her search.

MAN Find anything?

WOMAN No.

MAN Maybe a latch or a secret trap door?

WOMAN No, okay?

MAN A rabbit hole to lead us outta here?

WOMAN Don't you dare Alice in Wonderland me!

MAN Alison Enny!

WOMAN What?

MAN Enny. It's what I called you.

She hears her name as if for the first time.

I always loved your last name. With a Y. Loved saying it. Loved you.

WOMAN Look. I don't think we're here for some form of couple's therapy. Would you agree?

MAN I think that's a fair assessment.

WOMAN So you really don't need to do that.

MAN Do what?

WOMAN You know what.

MAN No I don't. Don't need to do what?

WOMAN That! That nostalgic... fishing-for-romance-holding-onto-the-memory   of-us thing.

MAN Hey, I'm just going off the faint light beam of memory I have that's waking in my shadowy mind. I'm responding to the memory of what I feel. What I knew. Doesn't it comfort you in any way to know I feel some fondness for you?

WOMAN Not really. I'm sorry. What am I supposed to say?

MAN Well... I'm sure the bad memories of who you really are or how you got like -

WOMAN Like what?

MAN This. I'm sure they'll come back too.

WOMAN The better the sooner.

MAN Don't make me feel bad for remembering the good in you. Shouldn't that tell you something, that that's the first thing?

WOMAN I'm not your memory of who I was.

MAN Then what are you?

WOMAN I'm - I'm not even what I can remember. I'M MORE THAN THAT! Or maybe I'm less. Forget it.

She pulls out the locket and examines it.

MAN I'm starting to wonder if I'm right that I married you.

WOMAN That's what we call the end of the honeymoon phase... honey.

MAN How do you think it broke?

WOMAN Probably the obvious contrasts in our personalities finally wore one of us down.

MAN No, I mean the locket.

WOMAN Oh. That's what I was wondering. A number of links are stretched like - I don't know - like a weight was pulled against them long enough to bend them. See?

MAN Huh.

She puts it around her neck.

WOMAN Strange, isn't it? What is this, silver?

MAN Looks like it to me.

WOMAN If it's real silver, it wouldn't be an easy thing to break, would it?

MAN Shouldn't.

WOMAN What?

MAN Nothing.

WOMAN Something's the matter, what is it?

MAN An incomplete thought... that these items are... artifacts

WOMAN Artifacts? What do you mean?

MAN That they're important, is all.

WOMAN Obviously.

MAN But like they're planted here for a reason. For us.

WOMAN Well no shit, Sherlock. You're just figuring that out now? You must've been a terror in the court room. Didn't we already agree on this? The lights, the sounds. They've been helping us piece things together all along.

MAN But I mean not just for us. Artifacts of some sort of record. Like a historical record - evidence.

WOMAN Evidence? Evidence of what? A crime?

MAN That we had some part in.

WOMAN I'm not a criminal!

At this phrase, a loud THUD and a succession of lights until now unseen, embedded in the pod, light up then go out.

MORE LIGHTS

MAN That's ominous. But not unfamiliar to me. I've seen that before. That pod light up like that before.

WOMAN I've seen it too.

MAN Then it is true.

WOMAN It can't be.

MAN There has been a crime.

WOMAN No, this can't be what this is.

MAN You know it is.

WOMAN No I don't. What I know is that I'm no criminal!

> *THUD. LIGHTS on the pod again.*

MAN You see? You've just confirmed it!

WOMAN There's been a mistake.

MAN We're Contestants!

WOMAN Shh!

MAN I might not remember much else, but I could

never forget that sound or those lights.

WOMAN I'm no -

MAN Stop! Don't say it -

WOMAN Criminal!

THUD. LIGHTS.

No! Stop!

MAN Everyone who says that is the one that usually dies!

WOMAN But I'm not!

MAN Settle down!

WOMAN I can't. I'll lose it!

MAN They won't let you.

WOMAN How could we have not seen this?

MAN No one ever does.

WOMAN The sound, the lights -

MAN It's not worth questioning

WOMAN These prison uniforms. The pod. What fools!

MAN It's the drugs, Enny. No one remembers. It's part of the game.

WOMAN This can't be real.

MAN It's why people watch. They would even if they had a choice.

He faces the unseen audience, body inhabited with anger.

It's why there are countless people watching us right now. Leaning forward in their chairs at home. Tuning in right now. Salivating for the first real smell of blood. You animals!

Turning to her.

They know one of us is dead. That our fate is sealed.

He becomes aware of the irony.

'Til death do us part.

WOMAN I'm no longer bound to those vows.

MAN Were you ever?

WOMAN I would like to hope so.

How does it work? I'm still foggy all over. How do we - how does one of us end up... [indicating the pod] there?

He gestures to where he perceives the audience to be.

MAN They decide.

WOMAN Who do they think they are to decide?

MAN Don't you see?

WOMAN No, that's why I'm asking.

MAN We've already been to trial.

WOMAN Where's our proof?

MAN This is it -

WOMAN Where?

MAN This. Us. Here - is your proof.

WOMAN Some proof. We're here. So what?

MAN Don't you remember how it works?

WOMAN Obviously not!

MAN When there's one person on the show, they're already guilty. The audience decides the way they die. When two people end up here... it means -

WOMAN Means what?

MAN Hung jury. But enough evidence to be sure -

WOMAN Sure about what?

MAN Sure that one of us committed the crime.

WOMAN For a lawyer you sure don't know how to convince someone.

MAN I didn't say I like it or that I agree with it. I didn't make the rules.

WOMAN Then who did?

MAN A suitcase nuke in Paris made that rule. A world on edge of slipping forever into constant anarchy made that law. One of us did something. Something bad.

WOMAN But I swore an oath! [Fighting to hold onto the memory] To hold him - Ah!

Head-splitting pain.

MAN To hold who?

WOMAN *To hold him who has taught me this art as equal to my parents and to live my life... for the benefit of the sick* - Yes! *According to my ability and judgment; I will keep them from harm and injustice.*

I'm remembering. See?

MAN Great.

WOMAN *I will neither give a deadly drug to anybody if asked for it, nor will I make a suggestion to this effect. In purity and holiness I will guard my life and my art.*

MAN So what's it supposed to mean to me?

WOMAN I swore an oath, in my profession.

MAN And you swore an oath to me once too.

WOMAN If the jury was hung, that means they couldn't decide beyond a shadow of a doubt. Isn't that tantamount to not proving guilt?

MAN After Paris, life as we know it went to hell.

WOMAN Life and our legal system.

MAN But don't you see. If we're here, if we're Contestants, we agreed to this.

WOMAN Are you crazy?

MAN We asked for this!

LIGHTS and a THUD.

How did we not see this?

RECORDING DEVICES

Upstage a sheen of glass creates a border. Behind the glass there are cameras, red lights on the multiple devices indicating every word, movement, reaction has been recorded.

WOMAN We're being watched.

MAN Of course we are.

WOMAN By who?

MAN Does it matter?

WOMAN It does to me! I never would've asked for this! Never!

MAN Of course not. But there wouldn't have been many options.

WOMAN Who's watching us?

MAN People, at home in their living rooms getting ready for dinner. Lovers sitting closely together on couches, who will make love at the end of the night and forget about us in the morning. People who need a thrill at the end of the work day and are scrolling their devices!

WOMAN And they're the ones who will vote. They'll choose our fate?

MAN It's coming back now, isn't it.

WOMAN This can't be!

MAN But it is.

She walks around the space, looking for a way out. While she does this, he goes and sits in the pod. After giving up frustrated she looks for him, sees him in the pod.

WOMAN What are you doing?

MAN What does it look like? I'm sitting.

WOMAN Get off of there!

MAN Why?

WOMAN Get off of that thing!

She walks over and grabs his arm. She tries to haul him up.

MAN Hey.

WOMAN Get up!

MAN Take it easy.

WOMAN Get off! You're not going to end it like that!

MAN Like what?

Her efforts to remove him are futile.

WOMAN You're not going to be a martyr!

MAN Martyr?

WOMAN You heard me. What are you trying to do, feign innocence. Is that your game?

MAN What game?

WOMAN Sitting down, offering your life again, trying to convince whoever's watching of your innocence by being willing to die.

MAN You're a real treat, aren't you?

WOMAN A murderous, child-killing treat.

MAN I didn't say that.

WOMAN But it's what you want them to think. Isn't it? You've been playing a game all this time, haven't you?

MAN no

WOMAN pretending you don't know what this is

MAN what are you talking about?

WOMAN pretending you can't remember who you are or where you are

MAN Enny

WOMAN Hah! Right there, see? Pretending you don't know my name

MAN stop this

WOMAN and not telling me yours. What is it, huh?

MAN I could say the same of you

WOMAN Not a chance.

MAN When I woke up

WOMAN This is all your ploy

MAN you were there watching me

WOMAN I have no idea - I had no idea about any of this!

MAN Oh? You were sitting there, watching me like a vulture, stooped, staring, planning out when to rip the flesh off my bones.

WOMAN I'm the vulture?

MAN Yeah, you are.

WOMAN I planned all this.

MAN Why not?

WOMAN Kill David, then pull off a hung jury so I could see you die in this forsaken place?

MAN A clever vulture. Wait. What did you say about David?

WOMAN Is that why we're here? We're here because they think one of us killed our son?

MAN There's a certain terrible feeling, hearing you say it out loud.

WOMAN Oh my.

MAN I just wanted to sit down. Alright?

WOMAN On that?

MAN To think. Can I do that? Can I think?

WOMAN I guess.

MAN Besides, the floor's cold.

> *She sits in the pod beside him. He moves so they can reasonably fit. It's tight*

Does that make me a devious murderer?

> *A quiet moment of being.*

Do you remember him?

WOMAN Who?

MAN Our son?

WOMAN Hmm. I can hardly see his face, hardly remember his little body.

MAN What do you remember?

WOMAN I can hardly make it out. I carried him inside of me for 9 months and I can barely remember the features of his face. Isn't that horrible?

MAN He had a scar.

WOMAN Where?

MAN Here [running his finger back and forth along her cheek bone, gently]. The shape of a little half moon. It raised up above his skin and was lighter than all the rest. Kind of like one I got, that you can see better when I haven't shaved for a few days. You would kiss it... his little scar.

WOMAN Every night, before he went to sleep.

MAN That's right. We hosted a party. It must've been his birthday. One of those theme things you liked to do.

WOMAN Themes?

MAN Yeah. There were probably 100 kids - most of 'em David didn't know - he was so shy. It was a Mexican theme.

WOMAN Mexican? You're making this up.

MAN No! Because there was a piñata.

WOMAN Who doesn't love a piñata?

MAN It was a ridiculous monstrosity of a piñata. You gotta remember it.

WOMAN I don't

MAN Come on... how can you not remember it?

WOMAN We're drugged. I can't remember your name.

MAN I think you're embarrassed and so you're pretending that you don't remember this thing.

WOMAN Why would I be embarrassed?

MAN Because it was your idea, first off. I don't know where in the world you found this thing, but it was one of the Three Amigos. You remember them, right? The Invisible Horseman. The Singing Bush.

WOMAN We loved that movie.

MAN I don't know which one it was, Chevy Chase or Steve Martin or Martin Short, but the piñata was one of the Three Amigos sitting backwards on his horse.

WOMAN Spurs and all.

MAN Exactly. Spurs and all.

WOMAN It's coming back.

MAN See! And David (laughing) he attacked that thing. There wasn't anything gonna stop him and he went after it swinging. Remember that? People were jumping out of the way as he swung at the air like a blindfolded gladiator out to club a baby seal.

WOMAN I can hardly imagine.

MAN And when he finally made contact with the darn thing he right took off the Amigo's head. But he hit so hard

WOMAN the whole piñata swung back toward him

MAN Right

WOMAN And the spur -

MAN A real spur -

WOMAN swung back and nicked his little cheek. Oh, the sweetheart.

MAN A real spur on a child's piñata. What were we thinking?

WOMAN Gosh. There was blood everywhere, wasn't there?

MAN Yep. And a hundred kids pounced on the Amigo head full of candy like a horde of hungry zombies. It was gory.

WOMAN I kissed him on the chin every night. Kissed that scar. "My little Amigo," I'd say, then turn off the light.

MAN He was a good boy, our boy.

WOMAN He was a good boy.

MAN What happened to us?

She stands up. Moves away from him.

I mean, how could it end like this... here? It just doesn't seem likely. Imagine our high school classmates out there, watching us. I mean, are they sitting there saying: "Yep, I called it"?

I love you.

She turns to him, perhaps in shock. Perhaps anger.

Or I did. I loved David. My memories - they're good memories. How could we have ever gone from there to here?

WOMAN I don't wanna know.

MAN You don't?

WOMAN No! Why?

MAN Because -

WOMAN Give me more drugs. Or turn off the lights - put me in that pod. I don't care. We lived all the pain of it once already. Why live it again?

MAN Why?

WOMAN Yes why ask to know?

MAN Because we need to know.

WOMAN I don't.

MAN I'm not afraid of the truth.

PAPER TRAIL

THUD. LIGHTS. Images are projected on a screen. He stands up. They both are drawn toward the images. They include news footage of the MAN and WOMAN during the trial as they are led into the courthouse.

Images of their home. Images of the school where the crime took place.

There are also newspaper clippings with their photos and headlines from the court hearing. Headlines flash:

Community rocked by school shooting

Families of victims mourn loss, point fingers

Friends of accused paint picture of happy family life, service to community

He said, she said: Couple facing murder charges caught in nasty divorce proceedings when son killed

Police Chief calls Wade child's death "Clear case of murder" still no formal charges against either parent

Grand Jury rules there is enough evidence to bring first-degree murder charges against parent of dead boy

Sleeping with the enemy: Spouse of accused to take stand in harrowing murder trial

Family heirloom cited as key evidence in first degree murder trial

Chemical traces, gas mask found near body of Wade child in explosive day of court proceedings

"Let 'em both fry": Brother calls for harsh sentence for his doctor sibling and her lawyer ex-husband

Sequestered jury enters Day 3 of deliberations as shocked nation holds breath

WOMAN This isn't a dream.

MAN No.

WOMAN There we are. I don't remember a thing from the trial. How can I not remember?

MAN That's part of it.

WOMAN I can't even defend myself.

MAN We're beyond that.

WOMAN But I don't know if I was on the witness stand or if I was the bloody accused!

MAN It doesn't matter -

WOMAN Doesn't matter? Only one of us could've been charged with murder.

MAN And there wasn't enough proof.

WOMAN It could've been a sham trial. You, the DA, all lawyered up, off on a technicality.

MAN If I was the accused. You, a doctor to children. You could hide the needle marks and the poison that killed David easy enough.

WOMAN How dare you accuse me!

MAN How dare you act so self-righteously, when we're both standing here like this.

The images disappear from the walls.

WOMAN [To whomever] Why don't you just flip your coin and get it over with!

MAN What's done is done.

WOMAN Oh yeah? So that's it? We just go to our fate?

MAN Look. We don't have to be at each other's throats.

WOMAN Well we don't have to go like lambs to the slaughter, either. But what has been done? Huh?

MAN I don't know

WOMAN Exactly!

MAN But whatever it was, I can't change it anymore, can you? Whether I want to or whether I even could, the thing is I can't.

WOMAN I can't even remember what occurred.

MAN But that doesn't change what you did or didn't do! What I've done or not done. One of us, you or me... the people who brought our son into the world, who were responsible for his life, we -

WOMAN If I can't remember, then how can I be held responsible? If I don't know what happened then how the hell can I regret?

MAN So forgetfulness is your absolution?

WOMAN Not of what was done, but can't it absolve me of whatever would stop me from saying that we still want him alive?

I can't tell you what I did! I can't tell you what happened to us. Does that mean I can't still want him alive? Can't I still love him?

She cries. Angry, sad, fighting. Relenting.

MAN We're responsible for what we do.

WOMAN I know that.

MAN Someone has to be held responsible for what was done to David.

WOMAN I know. I just don't see what it matters now.

She moves quickly to the pod. Sits in it, starts to strap herself in.

MAN Hey! What - no wait - what are you doing?

WOMAN I'm getting out of here.

MAN That's your plan now?

WOMAN Turn on the switch, boys!

MAN They can't.

WOMAN Nice knowing you

MAN They won't do it. It's out of our hands now. Don't you see? We've both done all we could do.

WOMAN How do you suddenly know so much?

MAN It's what this is. I don't know much, but I know enough to know that.

She winces in pain. Screams.

What is it?

WOMAN Memories! Ow ow ow.

MAN Memories of what?

WOMAN Oh, my head!

She regains composure. She is haunted by the vision she sees in her mind's eye.

WOMAN It was me.

MAN Is it still painful?

WOMAN I killed him.

MAN What?

WOMAN Do you hear me? It was me all along you naive little prick. I dragged you into it, and I tried to get away with it.

MAN You devil.

WOMAN You fool.

MAN Why?

WOMAN Why? Or how?

As she delivers the next lines it's as though she's giving the play-by-play to film footage of her memory.

WOMAN I was at home, alone... with David. And you - I... we were fighting. We were angry. It got so ugly. You couldn't be near me anymore. You would disappear. You were so... terrified. Still. So weak. And your weakness, it made me angrier.

MAN Angry enough to kill our little boy?

WOMAN I was being merciful.

MAN Merciful?

WOMAN Yes! To you. To us.

MAN Bullsh -

WOMAN You were right to be terrified. It was so dangerous then. Our neighbourhoods were locked down. Troops were in the streets.

MAN Because another bomb went off.

WOMAN Yes. In Beijing.

MAN "No more wall in China." I remember the headline in the Times.

WOMAN You thanked God that we weren't in Paris when the first bomb went off. Well I prayed the next one would hit Manhattan. Take us out. I hated what life had become.

MAN That's not like you. It's not the Dr. Enny I know.

WOMAN You can't remember that woman.

MAN Can you?

WOMAN Whoever I was, I changed.

MAN Into a murderer?

WOMAN I wasn't the only one. Gangs. Do you remember the gangs?

> *He grabs his skull in a sudden burst of pain.*

See, you're starting to.

MAN Ah ah ah!

WOMAN They started to take over the streets. Started plucking kids from schools, from malls. They started to make their own armies in the boroughs, to take over the city. Raced to get their own portable nukes. A terrifying tribalism started to take over the whole city in a matter of days.

MAN But it stopped.

WOMAN How could I know it would? David was too young to be part of any of it! I wouldn't let a gang steal his little life, to corrupt it!

MAN So you killed him?

WOMAN During one of the rolling power outages. The mandatory outages. It was so hot in the city, without air-conditioning. And the whole state was doing rolling brown outs, planned black outs. And I went to the school. Told him we'd sneak into the pool. And I...

MAN Say it

WOMAN I did it there. Face mask, goggles, everything. Just like I was one of the militant gang members.

MAN Made it look like a gang-nabbing gone wrong, when the school was vulnerable, during a power outage.

He walks away from her, to the edge of shadow, hides from her.

WOMAN Three days later there were two marines on every street corner in New York City. And every gang member was in a cell in Guantanamo. And David? He was gone.

MAN He grabbed your locket as he resisted. He tore it from your neck. That was the clue that solved the crime.

WOMAN Yes, he did.

He steps back into the light.

MAN Good story. You almost had me convinced. But it's not your real story.

WOMAN What?

MAN That's the story my lawyer presented at the trial, to the jury. The one you denied.

WOMAN But I saw it all, just there, when the pain came, almost knocked me to the floor. That's what I remembered.

MAN Your memory might be rebooting, but it's selectively presenting the facts.

She thinks about this. Fights against the restraints she's put herself in.

WOMAN End this! End me!

MAN Your life's no longer in your hands.

WOMAN How can this be justice?

MAN No one cares about that anymore. It's entertainment. All they want is a good show.

WOMAN So they'll be happy as long as one of us is euthanized and the other goes free?

MAN Something like that. As long as it feels like someone paid for something.

WOMAN What if they get it wrong?

MAN They already did. I don't believe there's a universe that exists in which either of us has done this.

WOMAN So how do we fight it? How do we make our case?

MAN It's too late.

WOMAN How do they get the... the chosen person - how do they get them in the pod

MAN They have a certain way. But you already volunteered.

She scrambles to get free.

What, now you're not so sure?

WOMAN How did you do it?

MAN Do what?

WOMAN How did you kill our son?

MAN That was a quick reversal. Where's the sudden attrition?

WOMAN That's not what I'm saying. How did my legal team explain your crime?

He bundles over in a sudden bout of pain. It is agonizing.

MAN David David DAVID!

WOMAN How are they triggering the memories? It is drugs, isn't it?

He grabs at his shirt, pulls it up, tears it off. He scratches at his body and contorts, finding a small bump under his shoulder. He presses it, kneads it.

MAN There.

She steps towards him, looks at it. Fingers the bump.

WOMAN It's some sort of slow release mechanism. Probably like an insulin pump that they can control remotely. Fascinating.

MAN We're getting closer to it now. Our story is almost up!

The pain stops. Wide-eyed he stares into a void.

WOMAN What did they say, what did my legal team bring before the judge?

MAN It was you that was on trial. Your team brought me to trial in the court of public opinion.

"In cold blood."

WOMAN Those were my words.

MAN All over the news.

He walks over to the gas mask.

Our sweet boy. He was found in the hallway, but they said he didn't die from a gun shot wound. That it was a poison that shut down his heart, that I made it look like a gang-inflicted wound ended his life.

WOMAN You wore the mask.

MAN There was residue of a nerve agent with my prints on the mask. DNA evidence.

WOMAN Premeditated.

MAN Cold blooded. And yet it's you who's the doctor, that works with drugs.

WOMAN I took an oath!

MAN You're the one who knows how to use the mask.

WOMAN So there were two ways he could've died but I orchestrated them both?

MAN There was the necklace!

WOMAN Which could break in a hundred ways.

MAN Bruising your neck where it was pulled.

WOMAN How conveniently you're remembering the facts. This has all been part of your elaborate scheme to see me fry. Well there we have it then. I've confessed and you've accused me. So I should sit back down and die.

Isn't it possible that there's a third option?

MAN If we're here, then no.

WOMAN Not another killer? Not some enemy who'd frame us?

MAN It'd be convenient.

WOMAN Not an accident?

MAN The jury was hung on the fact that one of us was the killer, but they couldn't decide.

WOMAN Mrs. Peacock in the bathroom with the nerve gas? Or wait, is it Professor Plumb? This isn't a bloody board game! This isn't some cute riddle to solve.

MAN One of us is guilty!

WOMAN In a justice system that's rigged for God-know's-what reason? To entertain the masses and keep them afraid? Locked in their homes in a world with nuclear bombs wiping out cities! Do you have any confidence in our system of laws— in our police state—to live or die by that?

MAN What I know is that we're here and David is not! God rest his soul.

She takes the gas mask from his hand and throws it at the chair.

WOMAN This is a mockery!

He walks to where the photos were left and picks them off the ground.

Tell me, if it's me they pick... if you live, will you be able to live with yourself?

MAN No.

He looks up from the photo.

Will you?

WOMAN I don't think so.

MAN Maybe that's your justice.

He hands her one of the photos. She takes it and looks at the child.

WOMAN I'm so sorry.

MAN He was beautiful.

He reaches for her hand.

He had your eyes.

WOMAN Can you promise me something.

MAN What?

WOMAN If you make it out of here alive, you won't rest until you find the truth.

MAN Yes.

She nods back. He holds her hand, facing her. She turns, facing the audience and looking to the spotlight.

WOMAN No more talking now. Let them decide.

He looks at her a moment longer, then turns to face the audience. Finally he looks at the light.

They both stand as if bracing themselves to be struck by a heavy blow, defiant, as though the blow once landed might not knock them down. Slowly all lights fade out to black but for one, which focuses on the signs with their numbers and the words WOMAN or MAN.

Their faces are suddenly lit in the dark. They are blinded. The red recording lights of cameras can be seen glowing in the perimeter.

A VOICE: Here's the moment you've all been waiting for. It's time to vote. You decide who lives and who dies.

END.

THE 49 - PREVIEW

*Read the first few parts
of the thrilling new series
by Andrew Kooman.*

*Subscribe to
The49.Substack.com to get
the story right in your inbox.*

**Forty-nine. The last President inaugurated in the
United States.**

The span of terrible days after the global

communications black out when the world was reshaped.

Forty-nine. The number of Phos—strange, supernatural phenomena—that appear in different geographic locations around the globe.

The critical parallel on what used to be the Canada-US border. Now the key power centre in Corridor West. A point on the map where the world's future seems to hinge.

Forty-nine.

The world is in a time of major turmoil ever since a suitcase nuke in Paris brought Europe to its knees and reshaped the world and its maps, governments, alliances.

Can a single nuke do that?

It wasn't just one. A secret organization of terrorists promised to inflict similar violence on major cities around the world. Beijing was next. Governments reeled. Not only to recover from the environmental fallout from Paris and Beijing, but from the economic destruction and social fragmentation. What materialized from the cloud of radioactive fallout was a new state of fear.

And opportunity.

While the relative peace of the last century is gone and the semblance and order, known throughout the 21st century, is a memory, there are some geographic areas where humanity thrives.

As the governments that survive became more authoritarian and the surveillance State becomes even more invasive, strange coalitions emerge. Globalism and economic nationalism collide with social justice warriors and vigilantes as old, tired political alliances fray.

Alliances that worked in the past fail. Identity groups and the new, unknown enemy threatening more attacks both remove and reshape lines of social and political division.

The US, with the help of NATO countries, scrambled to maintain its dominance and protect global assets, especially oil and water reserves which they feared would be the next target after the symbolic destruction of the City of Lights and the Empire that built the first Great Wall.

But it is the world's billionaires that are most ascendant.

Where governments fail due to faltering resourcing and mismanagement, billionaires with their tech companies and data-driven, direct-to-consumer infrastructure fill the gap and oversee entire regions of the globe. Their close relationship with former military, well-run NGOs, and private security companies, forged and tested through crises of the recent past– the Afghanistan withdrawl, Helene, LA's fires, Paris–demonstrate their unique abilities to help people in need, especially in times of trauma or emergency.

Especially after the population, worldwide, is decimated. High tech fiefdoms become havens for clusters of the world's remaining population.

With a social fabric so frayed it was inevitable that new territorial zones would emerge. Corridors around the world where those with resources and power make alliances with the citizenry to preserve a way of life. New North with its two Corridors: West and East. The New Soviet Corridor. Afrique. Asia Minor.

Canada, with its close proximity to the United States, becomes a major threat for the next nuclear strike. Rich in natural resources—especially oil, lumber and water —and due to the tech boom of the late 21st century in the Green Belt in Ontario, which was already a key centre of global data storage and digital infrastructure, the northern nation becomes a key political player and a satellite of a key billionaire alliance. Smart money from what used to be known as Silicon Valley.

The New North is a wild experiment—for humanity to survive, society had to be remade. And the off-world project of visionaries in tech and space push us closer to start new projects in the stars.

Can humanity thrive in these newly formed regions as it pushes lawlessness and political turmoil outside the walls of its corridors? Can it transport this new order and vision to colonize the stars?

Welcome to *The 49*.

She hadn't been outside the wall in months. Recently, it wasn't worth the risk. Or the hassle. First she'd been summoned. Now she was being sent.

One still had to marvel at the speed they built it. All those decades fighting about the wall on the southern border before Paris. When there were 50 States and a sovereign border between them and Mexico.

Is it humane? Who can come in and out?

As Boyer drove toward the eastern edge of Corridor West, the loud but almost forgotten voices of the recent past played in her mind. The Bishop mocked the bi-polar nature of the pundits, when there was still a thing called broadcast news. He told her how everyone who bickered and argued against enforcing borders, especially the ones who advocated for unlimited hospitality, didn't raise a single objection when they erected this wall.

Maybe they all were dead. Maybe they had a change of heart.

The border crisis. The housing crisis. The inflation crisis. Problems that seem almost luxurious. Wiped away, almost instantly, because of Paris.

The hand-wringing over who comes in, who stays out stopped. The gaslighting stopped. People shut their doors. Reached for guns. Welcomed the walls.

If you time traveled back to the turn of the century, the Bishop had said, *and asked someone where they expected the biggest wall to be built, surely they would have said between the US and Mexico along the natural barrier of the Rio Grande.* But they wouldn't have imagined Corridor West.

Developments in concrete 3D printing accelerated the ability to build big structures quickly, and that one wall so long the focus and crucible of political power, was now a corridor that shut out the rest of the world. A marvel to rival—perhaps even exceed—the wonders of the world ancient and the pre-Paris world which once had the Great Wall of China.

The size of it was staggering.

Boyer had only seen pictures online of the progress made from what used to be southern California up to the north of Canada. The dramatic line that shot straight up from San Diego and curved, an extended parenthesis carved as though by the finger of God in the stony tablet of the new world. With it an entire new law and set of rules for humanity.

That parentheses, half of a whole, reflected but also dwarfed a similar line in the East, if you zoomed out on the map of New North. The unfinished line of Corridor East that cut up from the eastern port of New York through Toronto and shot up north. The Great Lakes formed the natural, west-most barrier of the energy sector.

From that satellite view it all looked so simple, factual. The walls grew longer every day as concrete sections replaced the hovering drones which didn't move, just floated higher above the new structures, their multiple lenses pointed in every direction.

From space, it all looked so neat. As though the map were a casual afterthought, completing a long sentence in history. *Between order, darkness. Before progress, chaos.* An explanation to the passengers who launched off world. What was the message? *This is where it all ends up.*

Boyer checked the gauge on her dashboard. She would reach Maskwacis by dusk. There was enough charge.

The road was carefully protected from the air, but she couldn't help but double check every few miles.

Soon she'd be outside the wall. And a stone's throw from the Phos.

Diez tapped the ring on his right index finger against the fob. The flatscreen panel in what looked like a solid metal door appeared and scanned his face. At the prompt he leaned forward for the retinal scan.

By rote, he spread his arms and legs. Like Da Vinci's *Vitruvian Man*, he thought to himself. He couldn't help but wonder where the famous sketch by the artist ended up, or if it survived. It was traditionally housed in Venice. He knew that. Sometimes borrowed by the Louvre. *So much great art lost.*

As the pulse of the infrared camera dissipated, Diez returned his arms to his side, pulled from his thoughts when the green light framed the screen, his signal for all clear.

Nothing to hide.

A thought even the precise and invasive lenses and sensors couldn't detect. If they could, would they believe him? Would he believe himself?

Today's confession was in LA on the backlot of a

once great studio, where the big show was filmed. He preferred the lot in Calgary, which was closer to home. But he was itinerant and the Loop made for a fast trip.

He stepped through the door into the lobby. The entryway, geometric panes of glass restored since the looting and the fires that preceded them had almost put the city out for good, reflected light throughout the room. It reminded him of the great windows of Notre Dame for some reason, though there was no stained glass. The height, perhaps.

He stopped to look up at the light. Couldn't help himself. He let it seep into the skin. Penetrate the lines of his face. He stood there in a beam of sunshine palms out turned. Didn't care what the production staff buzzing to and from corridors that led to the sound stages might think.

He took a deep breath, aware he couldn't prepare for what the next few hours would bring. He would quiet his mind, even here. Especially here. He inhaled deeply, inhaled the earthy, welcome smell of the greenery in the lobby's atrium. Blossoms of an orange tree. The sharpness of fertilizer. Dirt.

He had stood like this, in Notre Dame. Eyes closed. Transported. The light through the glass of those windows had done it then. Years ago. When it reopened, after the fire that burned through it. Before it was lost, forever, along with everything else in that great city.

"Father Diez, welcome."

He opened his eyes. He didn't recognize the voice. The woman with the headset stood at a respectful distance, the impatience of a production manager: the ponytail quickly pulled into place, the half smile that turned down slightly at the corners of her mouth because the muscles were so used to frowning, her one flash of eye contact, then the return of her gaze to her watch.

"Ready for me?" he asked.

"Right this way." She was already walking. "The people have spoken."

***

He followed her through the lobby, past the reception area where the production crew came on break to grab a bite to eat, sit in the sun, gossip.

He could have walked it himself, he was familiar with the corridors, but it was a carefully guarded set, for good reason. As they approached the red room, they walked the gauntlet of souls—his term—the long corridor with photos of contestants on each side. Those who won and walked away. Those who did not. They looked at each other from their frames, the flat images in black and white more film noir portraits than mugshots.

Some of the most famous people in Corridor West, they were made up to look like movie stars. "No need to lead the witness," the show runner once said when he asked why they looked so glamorous. "It adds to the drama, and makes for great promo."

The necessary, ongoing evil of Corridor West. The terrible thread that wove through the new social fabric that kept it from ripping here. Stay in line, do your part, contribute and live a quiet life, and you'll do fine. Step out of line, you'll be gamed.

Justice turned over to the people, broadcast and streamed. Absolute.

Life is nasty, brutish and entertaining.

They walked in the direction of the sound stages, a maze of hallways that connected an intricate series of rooms where cameras rolled. He greeted the production assistants and crew with nods. Faces that were familiar. The people that made the game a reality.

The production manager knocked twice on a door and it hissed open. She nodded and was gone. He entered a room at the end of the hall after logging his arrival with a tap of his ring. There were two security personnel in this room. He smiled at them and they nodded back, not a word exchanged.

He knew the routine.

Priests and other so-called holy women and men throughout the centuries had different rituals associated with their orders and practices, some more elaborate than others.

He thought of the order of Levites. All the men of the priestly tribe were washed, dressed, anointed with oil in front of the tabernacle when they were first ordained. Before they entered the service they placed their hands on a bull before it was sacrificed. Followed by two rams. Offerings. Absolution.

Together they would make a meal of one of the rams, the ram of ordination. *But an outsider shall not eat of it.* Only the high priest could enter the holy place.

The inner sanctum of the terrible gameshow had, for better and for worse, become one of the main shared experiences for the people of Corridor West. A shared social experiment. A secular sacrament, so to speak. And here he was in the middle of it.

He'd quickly developed his own little ritual. He was aware with each movement of the emptiness of the rituals people perform in front of others who don't understand them or adhere to the system of worship they represent. Outward acts of performative religion.

First he removed the ring from his right index finger.

Without it, he and most anyone else in Corridor West were invisible. Not entirely. But nearly. It was the quickest identifier and tracker. Key and meal ticket. Opener of doors and acquirer of food and other life-sustaining resources. And the first line of defense against sickness. It monitored key biometrics through a series of sensors against the skin.

Next was the ring on his left index finger. The earthly possession that meant most to Diez. He turned it once, massaged the kub of bone above and below the metal, slowly worked it over his knuckle. He placed it gently in the plastic container beside the other ring.

He looked at the male guard after he put it down. The man nodded back.

Diez pulled his phone out next, from the inside pocket of his coat and placed it in a bin. Then he removed his coat, unlaced his boots and removed his socks. He had flashbacks to the days when air travel in airplanes was the main mode of transit for long distances. The long lines of airport security ended in the inconvenient, even ridiculous removal of shoes, boots, liquids, pens. How antiquated that seemed now.

But it stopped there, at the removal of boots and belts. Here, in the quiet rooms of the studio complex, he slipped off his shirt and undid his pants. He dropped them in a larger bin beside the ring.

He looked at the security guards again. Both the woman

and the man had bored looks on their faces. Two people whose names he didn't know who knew his body more intimately than any other human on the planet. Despite their bored expressions he noticed they both looked, reflexively, at his abdomen.

He stood in his underwear with only a wooden cross around his neck. A gold square was laid into the wood at the centre, connecting the vertical and horizontal beams. In the centre of the gold was a red ruby. The cross was attached to a green cord that hung to his abdomen, between his sternum and belly button. It rested on a scar that time had not healed. It was raw, like the wet skin of a tongue. He never got used to the sight of it himself, if he happened to see himself in a mirror.

His stomach was flat, chiseled even. *Intaglio.* Like a hand had carved sharp lines into his torso. The food shortages had weaned Corridor West of excesses that bloated so-called *developed* populations for centuries. But the muscle was also part of his assignment. It helped ratings, he was told. So to get his full rations he had to keep to a fitness routine.

The scar created a strange contrast to the cut of his stomach, like a sculptor had mixed mediums, added a wet entrail of clay in bas relief, that protruded at his oblique muscle and whipped up to his rib cage. A startling line, further contrasted by the wooden crucifix and green cord holding it in place.

The security personnel knew not to ask for him to remove it. They knew the routine as well.

But he did remove it, after dramatically crossing himself and whispering a prayer in Latin. He held the crucifix to his forehead, kissed it, then carefully lifted it from his neck. He placed it beside the rings, as though he were putting down a newborn in its crib, careful not to wake it.

To Diez, it was the most ridiculous part of the whole performance, but to the guards it always seemed to convey the most significant part of the charade that was the show. The performance of Corridor West.

He inwardly chastised himself. *Forgive me*. The cross still meant something. Even here. To him. He'd have to think about that, later, when he could contemplate.

He opened his hands to both guards and smiled. There was nothing left. They nodded at him and signaled for him to walk through the scanner. When he turned to walk through the sensors, they saw the burn marks and scars on his back. Enough to make someone wince at first look. But these guards didn't flinch.

Of course the scanners could sense any contraband he or anyone else might try to smuggle into the chamber beyond the doors. But this was all part of the show. The film crew, hidden in the shadows on the other side of the doorway, would capture the moment he walked through the door. The priest, stripped down and vulnerable, just like the contestant, there to deliver the last rites to whoever it was behind the door.

It was the big reveal of every final episode. Who got the vote. Who would live and who would die. And the strange story of his body, what it told to the camera— the vitality, the tragedy lived out by a priest of all people —helped set up the high stakes of the climax of every show, when the camera punched in and captured the look on the person behind the door who, like the rest of the viewing audience, was learning their fate live, in that very moment.

She was almost there now. She noted how tense she felt in her shoulders as though she'd been commandeering the vehicle, keeping it on the road. She wasn't.

It was a self-driving EV with a simple task. It was a straightforward route and carefully guarded. Most people inside and outside the walls agreed that it didn't require the protection of the Gov and his surveillance drones. Or the heavily armed troop of robotic soldiers on the convoy. Or heavily armed human soldiers with body armour and AR-15s.

Not since Bayankhongor.

Security forces from the New Soviet Corridor sent

drones and soldiers to take control of the Phos that appeared on the edge of the Gobi desert in the forgotten Mongolian district. The idea was to penetrate the phosphorescent fog, establish a perimeter.

Only the men and women of the security forces walked away.

Every weapon, every flying drone, every droid, including droid dogs simply powered down. Stopped working. Couldn't be revived or rebooted, even when transported back to home base.

Until that first Humbling, the powers of the Corridors seemed absolute, and the terrifying combination of human security forces and intelligent robots on land and air were unstoppable.

But Bayankhongor showed the world manmade powers were no match.

Boyer traveled with the type of security detail that the billionaires brought with them when they traveled. But now they were protecting food. And battery packs. There were other essentials, but those were the commodities most needed and most desired.

Boyer was sure she could've walked the road, unarmed, with the supplies, and the Surge wouldn't try to touch her. They knew its final destination. A few miles from Wetaskiwin, which was not far south of what used to be Edmonton, as the drone flies. Phos North, which dropped in Maskwacis. No Corridor on earth would allow a Surge to attempt an attack near a Phos.

It still didn't seem possible that something so good could fall there. It made sense to no one, least of all her. Not after what she'd seen. But no one could explain the Phos. Or control it. Not even the Gov.

What was his connection there? She couldn't make sense of it. The least likely place for the supernatural appearance. Nothing should surprise her but this did.

When she was summoned to the headquarters, the last thing she expected was to be sent home. And now she was helping to bring food outside the wall, into the Surge. Off the grid.

Boyer was pulled out of her thought by the familiar sound of a takeover notification. All the screens in the cab of the EV lit up with the familiar jingle of the game. The phone in her pocket buzzed and the screen lit up. *A reveal.*

She knew that every screen in the corridor was taken over at this very moment to broadcast the scene. She didn't like to, but she watched as the father materialized on screen. First just his face.

The camera punched in. The crows feet around his eyes revealed a man familiar with sorrow and with laughter.

The camera was unforgiving, but not unkind. It hid

nothing as he braced himself for the moment that the waiting audience wanted most, the punch out, before the side-by-side shot of the priest as his presence was revealed to the contestant about to learn their fate.

It was always a tense and potent moment. The priest would materialize and then step into the room to either give the contestant clemency or administer last rites. The viewing audience learned the fate along at the same time as the accused. Peak streaming.

He looked worn and dignified, even afraid. Kind. A mystery.

The show never shared his voice or gave his name, only showed him at the reveal in this close up shot. It was a smart choice, Boyer thought. Before the editors cut to the split screen, the audience couldn't help but imagine they were on the other side of that gaze.

The camera held tight to his face then suddenly punched back so that he was visible from the waist up, the gold square glimmering from the wooden cross that seemed immovable against the chiseled abs. The ruby alive with light, like a rounded drop of blood, a ripening grape.

Last rites. Boyer felt the wave, the endorphin rush this moment always delivered, no matter how many times she watched. The communal moment every person in Corridor West shared as they realized another Contestant's fate. Relief, surprise, dread, and what, *desire*? She felt a hot rush of shame.

He was the most popular priest, for obvious reasons. The fan fiction about him and what the women and men of Corridor West wanted to do with him popular on chat threads of the game show made her blush. He was onscreen for more reveals than any other priest.

The only way to find out what he said in that room was to sit in the judgment seat. And no one wanted that. No matter what the fan fiction fantasized.

Just as Boyer started to imagine what it would be like to touch his hand, the screen split and the lights on the right side of the screen flooded to reveal the condemned. A woman in white shorts and a white undershirt restrained in a chair.

Her red hair fell to her shoulders and after the shock of the light subsided, she screamed. The side-by-side image of his face and her terror was the reason for the takeover. It rightly put the fear of God and the state and the Gov in everyone's mind.

Another beep and the takeover was almost done. A confession booth materialized behind her. The priest stepped behind the accused and stepped into his place in the booth. Boyer and anyone else in Corridor West could go back to their business and would wait until the confession was over, the private, unseen moments between the accused and the priest before the final vote when the audience would decide the way the condemned would die and another takeover would occur so that everyone would witness what happens to anyone who disrupts the order of the Corridor.

Boyer looked out the window.

The thin thread of the northern lights danced above her in the sky. They'd been more active since the Phos arrived. But she barely noticed them. All she could think about was the priest and the crucifix that rested against his torso.

She had held that very cross in her own hands.

ABOUT THE AUTHOR

Andrew Kooman

Andrew Kooman is an award-winning writer and producer whose stories have touched and inspired millions of people around the world.

His work includes the critically acclaimed stage play We Are the Body, which toured Western Canada, the dramatic thriller She Has A Name, and the new book of poetry and prose The Many Dreams of Joseph which explores the different Josephs in the Bible.

Andrew's work explores the collisions of faith, justice and creativity in the real world, subjects he writes about on his popular Substack newsletter Things I Wrote Down.

Andrew co-founded Unveil Studios and the streaming

platform UnveilTV with his visionary brothers, the film directors Matthew and Daniel Kooman. Through Unveil, Andrew has travelled the world and produced documentary and feature films, including the original series Dream and Breath of Life.

Andrew lives near London, Ontario with his wife and two children. He works with an international non-profit that helps children and communities overcome generational poverty. He also makes people laugh in church across North America as an official author with the US theatre sensation the Skit Guys.

You can learn more about his writing at andrewkooman.com

PRAISE FOR AUTHOR

*She Has A Name is "a riveting, fast-paced political thriller."
- Calgary Herald "She Has A Name is a hugely important
film, bringing home the realities of a global issue that must
be tackled.*

- HER ROYAL HIGHNESS, PRINCESS EUGENIE OF YORK

*She Has A Name "offers a unique and timely perspective
into the realities of [human trafficking]."*

- CANON ANDREW WHITE, 'VICAR OF BAGHDAD'

*She Has A Name is a film of depth and detail, honestly
portraying how countless people lose life and liberty to
ruthless criminals.*

*- KEVIN HYLAND, OBE, THE UNITED KINGDOM'S FIRST
INDEPENDENT ANTI-SLAVERY COMMISSIONER*

BOOKS BY THIS AUTHOR

She Has A Name

In the dark world of Bangkok crime it's dangerous to trust anyone.

Jason, a human rights lawyer, poses as a john so he can secretly meet with a young woman known only as Number 18, forced to work as a prostitute in Bangkok's busy red light district.

But can he win 18's trust and convince her to risk her life to testify against her cut-throat pimp?

With a storyline ripped from today's headlines, SHE HAS A NAME is a page-turning thriller.

As Jason's investigation zeroes in on The Pearl, a popular destination for sex tourists from around the world, he becomes convinced that 18's testimony could be the key to solving a shocking crime that occurred on the Thai border.

Described as a "heart-breaking hit" (Calgary Sun) and "absolute must-see" (Ignite 107) critics across North America raved about SHE HAS A NAME.

Based on the thrilling stage play, The published script is now available for the first time in paperback, since touring Canada and being produced off-Broadway.

Delft Blue

When Holland falls to the Nazis in May of 1940 after a brief but surprising resistance, Machiel and Sophia van Leeuwen prepare for a long and difficult occupation in a war Holland never dreamed it would enter. Along with their 12-year-old daughter Johanna, they are soon faced with impossible decisions: to choose between resistance and passivity, family and friendship, and whether or not the sincere faith they've observed with its quiet traditions might now require unthinkable violence.

The award-winning script from playwright Andrew Kooman is a thrilling story about a tight-knit family who wrestle to live out their quiet, humble faith in a time that seems to require violence to stop the forces that oppose them.

Ten Silver Coins: The Drylings Of Acchora

"Refreshingly original!" -- Red Deer Express

"An excellent tale of second chances and acceptance, no matter where you come from or what your past may be." -- Associated Content

When she runs away from the city of Vendor, Jill Strong was only known as a Daughter of Disgrace. Everything changes when she flees to the Forest and is given a treasure - ten silver coins - which she quickly loses.

It's up to Jill and Simon, the boy she meets in the Forest, to recover the treasure. To do so, the children enter Acchora, a world inhabited by the Drylings who hide in the belly of a dormant volcano under the curse of the Rashtakar, the cruel being who seeks the very treasure Jill has lost.
In Vendor, imagination and adventure are forbidden. In Acchora, without them, Jill and the Drylings have no hope for survival.

From the imagination of award-winning author and playwright Andrew Kooman comes a thrilling new adventure series children of all ages will love, and families can read aloud together.

Perfect for readers' groups and book clubs that enjoy talking about adventure, the meaning of life, and what it means to be courageous in the world.

Ten Silver Coins: The Battle For Acchora

Critics are calling the highly anticipated second novel in Andrew Kooman's Ten Silver Coin series "a rich, adventurous tale."

The world's on fire and Jill strong set it aflame when she obeyed King Eckwith's dying wish to trigger the volcano. As she escapes with the Drylings from their hiding place into the land of Acchora, she's about to go from one dangerous realm into another.

With Juria now Queen over a divided nation, to survive above ground the Drylings must unite against the Rashtakar's armies that begin to fill the land. But Ama's discovery of wingless refugees on the slope of the burning mountain and a mysterious visitor from a far-away land threaten to further divide the Drylings into factions. The battle for Acchora is a fight not only for survival but for the future.

Even though Jill and Simon are outsiders caught up in the middle of the drama, without them, the battle for Acchora could be lost.

From the imagination of award-winning author and playwright Andrew Kooman The Battle for Acchora is a book loved by children and adults alike... and families can read and enjoy together.

Perfect for readers' groups and book clubs that enjoy talking about adventure, the meaning of life, and what it means to be courageous in the world.

"Hints of... legendary authors like C.S. Lewis, Madeleine L'Engle and J.R.R. Tolkien....What sets the book apart is Kooman's gift for painting pictures [with] words." - Red Deer Express

God / He

A collection of vivid, image-based poems, God/he is both love song and shouting match, a struggle between human and Divine. Through the collection /he faces the agony and insanity of existence head on as /he starts to become more unfamiliar with the God/ we all think we know so well: a God who is slippery as a fish, a trickster and green-thumb, a bloodhound on the hunt.

The book includes the award-winning poems three snapshots of the Trinity upon Christ's death on the cross, he's a miserable being, love, from the looks of it, he could kill you, he is capable, you put your thumb on it, and what confidence.

www.ingramcontent.com/pod-product-compliance
Lightning Source LLC
Chambersburg PA
CBHW060354180626
46817CB00008B/3013